CAMDEN COUNTY LIBRARY
203 LAUREL ROAD
VOORHEES, NJ 08043

0500000878739 7

W9-CFQ-632

JUN 0 6 2016

SUN ABOVE AND BLOOMS BELOW

A Springtime of Opposites

Felicia Sanzari Chernesky
Illustrated by Susan Swan

Albert Whitman & Company
Chicago, Illinois

For every egg in my nest—big, little, smooth,
and slightly cracked—FSC

For the most wonderful TRR, who endures all—SS

Also by Felicia Sanzari Chernesky and Susan Swan:
Sugar White Snow and Evergreens: A Winter Wonderland of Color
Cheers for a Dozen Ears: A Summer Crop of Counting
Pick a Circle, Gather Squares: A Fall Harvest of Shapes

Library of Congress Cataloging-in-Publication Data is on file with the publisher.

Text copyright © 2015 by Felicia Sanzari Chernesky
Illustrations copyright © 2015 by Susan Swan
Published in 2015 by Albert Whitman & Company
ISBN 978-0-8075-3632-2

All rights reserved. No part of this book may be reproduced or transmitted in any
form or by any means, electronic or mechanical, including photocopying,
recording, or by any information storage and retrieval system,
without permission in writing from the publisher.

Printed in China.
10 9 8 7 6 5 4 3 2 1 HH 20 19 18 17 16 15 14

For more information about Albert Whitman & Company,
visit our web site at www.albertwhitman.com.

"What daffodils!" Miss Ava cheered.
"The earth just blooms this time of year!
Cooped up **in** school, without a doubt,
you've caught spring fever.
We're going **out**."

"Take **off** your smocks and wash those hands.
Put **on** your slickers. We have great plans.

Our field trip will be so much fun.
We'll see chicks hatch. Please **walk**—don't **run**."

We climbed into the **empty** bus
and filled it **full** of all of us.

Waving as we passed through town,

we soared **up** hills

and flew back **down.**

From **far** away a weather vane
led us down a **crooked** lane,
past **straight** wood fences, squat red pens.

We parked **near** barns and clucking hens.

Such funny birds! Some **big**, some **small**,
fluffy, feathered, **short**, and **tall**.

A rooster crowed **atop** the coop.
At the **bottom**,
chicken poop!

We giggled with our field trip buddies.
The ground **below** our boots was muddy.

Above, a sky of **cloudy** gray
drizzled on our **sunny** day.

Miss Ava said,
"Now, don't complain.
It's just a little April rain!"

Then Lily played the traffic cop.
"The geese can **go**
but you must **stop**."

A sign hung on the **closed** barn door:
Open *me. Come in. Explore.*
An old **round** wheel was nailed beside
the small **square** window. We went inside.

Our slickers were **wet**, the hay bales **dry**.
Two barnyard mousers loafed nearby.
"The **white** cat's name is Whisker Jack,"
the farmer said. "And Buster's **black**."

We crowded around the incubator.
It warmed so **many** eggs! And later...

we noticed cracks in just a **few**.
What were those eggs about to do?

Miss Ava hushed us. "Listen! Watch!"
Peck-peck-peck—a chip, a notch...

Some eggs stayed **whole**.
Some eggs were **broken**.
The hatching newborn chicks had woken!

The farmer beckoned. "Soon enough, these **fragile** chicks are **sturdy** puffs." We laughed to see them nestling, **sleeping** and wide **awake**. Chicks hopping, peeping!

Miss Ava cried, "How time does fly!"
We thanked the farmer and waved **good-bye**.
Hello, blue skies and fresh, clean air!
Spring opposites are everywhere!

From **rain** to **shine** with room to roam,
our day **away** now led us **home**.